This book belongs to

On the Way Home

First published 1982 by Macmillan Children's Books
This revised edition published 2007 by Macmillan Children's Books
an imprint of Pan Macmillan,
a division of Macmillan Publishers Ltd
20 New Wharf Road, London N1 9RR
Associated companies throughout the world
www.panmacmillan.com

ISBN: 978-0-230-01584-5

Copyright © Jill Murphy 1982 and 2007

13 15 16 14

A CIP catalogue record is available for this book from the British Library.

Printed in China

On the Way Home

JILL MURPHY

MACMILLAN CHILDREN'S BOOKS

Claire had a bad knee, so she set off home to tell her mum all about it.

On the way home Claire met her friend Abigail.
"Look at my bad knee," said Claire.
"How did you do it?" asked Abigail.

"*Well,*" said Claire, "there was a *very* big, bad wolf,

and it came sneaking up behind me as I passed by, and it tried to take me home for its tea!

But I screamed for help and a woodcutter came and chased the wolf away,

and the wolf dropped me,
and *that's* how I got my bad knee."

"Gosh!" said Abigail.

Then Claire met her friend Paul.
"Look at my bad knee," said Claire.
"How did you do it?" asked Paul.

"*Well,*" said Claire, "there was
a *vast* flying-saucer,

and it came zooming out of the sky and tried to carry me off to a distant planet!

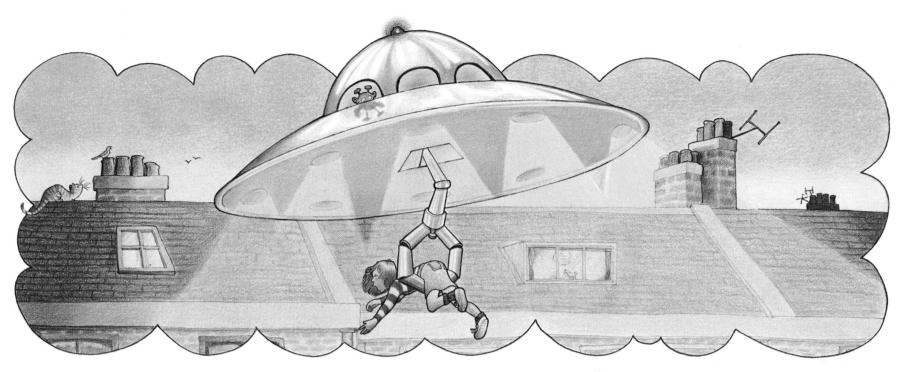

But I struggled free just in time and fell crashing to the earth far below,

and *that's* how I got my bad knee."

"Good gracious *me*!" gasped Paul.

Then Claire met her friend Amarjit.
"Look at my bad knee," said Claire.
"How did you do it?" asked Amarjit.

"*Well,*" said Claire, "there was a huge, hungry crocodile,

and it came lumbering out of the canal as I passed by, and it tried to pull me into the water.

But I crammed a piece of wood between its jaws and it was *so* cross that

it knocked me over with its tail,
and *that's* how I got my bad knee."

"How dreadful!" said Amarjit.

Then Claire met her friend Robert.
"Look at my bad knee," said Claire.
"How did you do it?" asked Robert.

"*Well*," said Claire,
"there was a big, fat snake,

and it came slithering out of a tree, and it wrapped itself around me,

and it *squeezed* and squashed! But I tickled it until it couldn't stop laughing

and it dropped me,
and *that's* how I got my bad knee."

"I *say*!" gasped Robert.

Then Claire met her friend Samantha.
"Look at my bad knee," said Claire.
"How did you do it?" asked Samantha.

"*Well*," said Claire, "there was
an enormous dragon,

and it came soaring out of the clouds, and it picked me up in its claws!

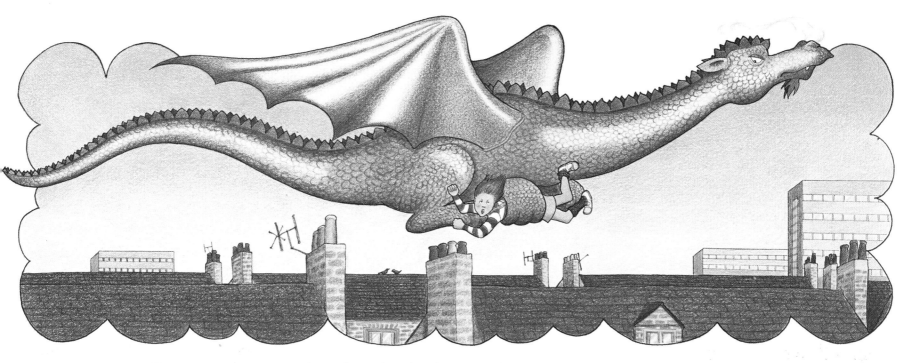

But I gave it such a big kick that it dropped me, and I fell for *miles*

and *miles* through the air,
and that's how I got my bad knee."

"Cor!" cried Samantha.

Then Claire met her friend Nick.
"Look at my bad knee," said Claire.
"How did you do it?" asked Nick.

"*Well,*" said Claire, "there was
a great, hairy gorilla,

and it came creeping out of a garage as I passed by, and it tried to drag me away!

But I stamped on its toe *so* hard that it let me fall to the ground with a bump,

and *that's* how I got my bad knee, *and* I didn't cry."

"Crumbs!" said Nick.

Then Claire met her friend Celia. "Look at my bad knee," said Claire. "How did you do it?" asked Celia.

"*Well*," said Claire, "there was a gigantic giant,

and he came stamping through the houses, and he picked me up and said,

'Fee fie foe fum, a tasty girl for my hungry tum!' But I punched him on the nose *so* hard

that he let me fall,
and *that's* how I got my bad knee."

"Well I *never*!" exclaimed Celia.

Then Claire met her friend Jonathan.
"Look at my bad knee," said Claire.
"How did you do it?" asked Jonathan.

"*Well,*" said Claire, "there was a ghastly ghost,

and it came gliding out of a gloomy graveyard as I passed by, and it went

'*WOOOOOOOOO*!'   But I ran away *so* fast that I left it behind, and then I tripped over,

and *that's* how I got my bad knee."

"Wow!" said Jonathan.

Then Claire met her friend Hannah.
"Look at my bad knee," said Claire.
"How did you do it?" asked Hannah.

"*Well*," said Claire, "there was
a wicked old witch,

and she came swooping down from the rooftops and bundled me into her shopping bag!

But I broke the bag with my feet and dived out onto the hard pavement,

and *that's* how I got my bad knee."

"Dear me!" exclaimed Hannah.

Claire arrived home and her mum came out.
"Look at my bad knee," said Claire.
"How did you do it?" asked her mum.

"*Well*," said Claire, "I was
in the playground

and I was having *such* a nice time on a swing, when *suddenly*, *suddenly* ———

I fell off!" Claire burst into tears.

"Never mind," said her mum. "Come inside and we'll put a plaster on it."

"A very *big* plaster?" asked Claire.   "The biggest in the whole box," said her mum.

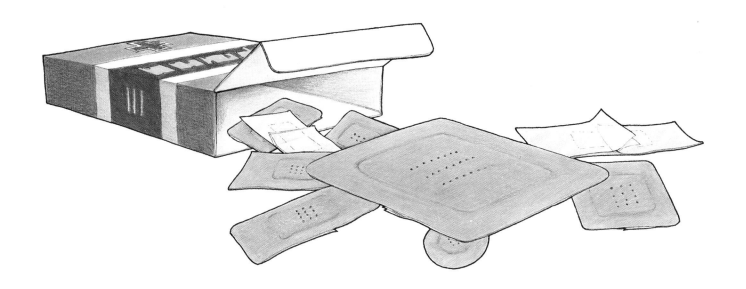